For Jack and Anna
MM

For Nigel and Annie
AA

ORCHARD BOOKS
Carmelite House, 50 Victoria Embankment, London EC4Y 0DZ
ISBN 978 1 84121 080 3
First published in 2001 by Orchard Books
First published in paperback in 2002
Text © Margaret Mayo 2001
Illustrations © Alex Ayliffe 2001
The rights of Margaret Mayo to be identified as the author
and of Alex Ayliffe to be identified as the illustrator of this
Work have been asserted by them in accordance with
the Copyrights, Designs and Patents Act, 1988.
A CIP catalogue record of this book is available from the British Library
25 24 23 22 21
Printed in China
Orchard Books is an imprint of Hachette Children's Group
Part of The Watts Publishing Group Limited
An Hachette UK Company
www.hachette.co.uk

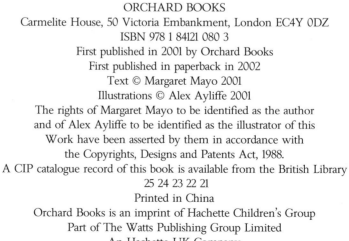

MIX
Paper from
responsible sources
FSC® C104740
FSC
www.fsc.org

Dig

Dig

Digging

Dig Dig Digging

written by
Margaret Mayo

illustrated by
Alex Ayliffe

ORCHARD

Diggers

Diggers are good at **dig**, **dig**, **dig**ging,
Scooping up the earth and lifting and tipping,
They make huge holes with their **dig**, **dig**, **dig**ging;
They can work all day.

Fire Engines

Fire engines are good at race, race, racing,
Nee-nar! Nee-nar! Bright lights flashing,
Hoses at the ready for swoosh, swoosh, swooshing;
They can work all day.

Tractors

Tractors are good at pull, pull, pulling,

Ploughing up the field with a squelch, squelch, squelching,

Round go the wheels, see the mud flying!
They can work all day.

Rubbish Trucks

Rubbish trucks are good at gobble, gobble, gobbling,

Crunching messy rubbish bags, squeezing and squashing,

Busy, busy rubbish-eaters, always gobbling;

They can work all day.

Cranes

Cranes are good at
lift,
lift,
lifting,
Up go the bricks
to the
top of
the building,

Down come the pipes,
very
slowly
spinning;
They
can
work
all day.

Transporters

Transporters are good at car transporting,
Ramps down, ramps up, shiny cars loading,
All aboard! Off they go -

vroom-vroom-vrooming;
They can work all day.

Dump Trucks

Dump trucks are good at dump, dump, dumping,
Carrying heavy loads and tip, tip, tipping,
Out fall the rocks -

CRASH!

- rumbling and tumbling;
They can work all day.

Rescue Helicopters

Helicopters are good at whirr, whirr, whirring,
Hovering and zooming, rotor blades whizzing.
Down comes the rope. Look! Someone needs rescuing!
They can work all day.

Road Rollers

Rollers are good at roll, roll, rolling;
Pressing hot sticky tar, smoothing and spreading,
Flattening the new road and slowly rolling;
They can work all day.

Bulldozers

Bulldozers are good at push, push, pushing,
Over rough, bumpy ground, scraping and shoving,

Caterpillar tracks are grip, grip, gripping;
They can work all day.

Lorries

Lorries are good at l o n g - d i s t a n c e travelling,
Long ones, tall ones, different loads carrying,
Hooting their horns – beep-beep! Their big wheels turning;
They can work all day.

What a busy day, now it's time for resting,
Brakes on, engines off, the sun is setting;
No beep-beeping, no vroom-vrooming –
Sshh!
They can rest all night.